Sleeps With The Fishes

J. Kevin Burchfield

This book is a work of fiction. Places, events, and situations in this story are purely fictional. Any resemblance to actual persons, living or dead, is coincidental.

No part of this book may be reproduced, stored in a retrieval system, or transmitted by any means without written permission of the author.

Copyright © 2016 J. Kevin Burchfield

All rights reserved.

ISBN: 13:9781523349685
ISBN-10:1523349689

DEDICATION

This book is dedicated to Cindy, Moose, Whiskey, Remington, Barley, and Monopoly Burchfield and my mother Lynda Burchfield.

CONTENTS

	Acknowledgments	I
1	First Trip of the Season	3
2	The Tip	14
3	The Talk	25
4	The Phone Rings	32
5	The First Job	36
6	A Few Good Days	46
7	The New Halibut Hole	50
8	Planning Ahead	57
9	Three Times The Fun	61
10	Busy Couple Of Days	64
11	Getting To Me	87
12	Facetime	90

13	JD Calls Again	96
14	O Captain, My Captain	100
15	Plans And Dreams	108
16	The Photographers	111
17	The Exit Strategy	118
18	The Next Chapter	130

ACKNOWLEDGMENTS

I would like to thank my wonderful wife Cindy for all of her hard work on this book in the realm of editing and as my sounding board. She inspires me every day and without her none of my dreams could ever come true.

I would also like to thank my dear friends Tori, Lenelle, Dan, and Daren for all of their support and inspiration.

In loving memory of Reid O. Mullins

First Trip Of The Season

I really am the luckiest dude on the planet! I have the most wonderful wife in Cindy...a great dog in Moose...many great friends and I get to take people fishing and whale watching in Alaska! I actually get paid for this stuff! It's crazy! Living large and feeling blessed!

Who am I you ask...well Capt. Kevin Burchfield of course! I'm the dude pictured on the front and back of all of my company's shirts! That's right...captains have no ego! And I've been fishing these waters for twenty years or so...livin' the dream!

The season is booking out nicely...just put the boat in the water a couple of weeks ago and ready for the first king salmon trip of the year.

It's May in Juneau so mornings are crisp and the sun...when we are fortunate enough to actually see that beautiful bright orb...is warm and bright. The mountains still are covered with snow and the contrast of the green trees with that snow makes for the most perfect vision! This truly is God's country!

To say that I'm a little excited about the first trip of the season would be an understatement! I am ready to go and I really want to kill some fish today! It's been way too long since there was blood on the deck...oh yeah fish are gonna die! But I do have to temper myself some...it is May and the fish are just starting to come back so we may be going for a nice boat ride! Still I know that the only way to guarantee that one does not catch a fish is to not go fishing! We are definitely gonna give it hell today!

Loaded up the old truck with my bait bag and gear bag and took off for the dock.

Stopped at the coffee shop for my chai tea and to chat up the cuties that work there…it's a required thing…not the tea…chatting up the cuties! We old guys know how to do this way better than the young guys! I've seen my deckhands try…stumble…and fail and then I swoop in and save the day and hook up the goofy deckhand with said cutie! Ah…but I digress!

With said chai tea on board I make my way to the local convenience store Breeze Inn to grab some ice and sandwiches for our trip. Oh and chat up these ladies as well!

Then off to the dock! Once there I load up my cart…yes my cart…the one with my face all over it! Do not even think about touching my cart…oh that really pisses me off! Anyway…then I make my way down to the boat. Stopping briefly to talk to Capt. Ben Olson to see if he has a fish report.

Ben is a lot like me...loud and obnoxious in an endearing way! We both tend to be larger than life and always the center of attention. My wife blames my mother for not having any other children...yep I'm an only child and I like being the center of attention! None of us are sure just who to blame for Ben! He's a good guy and a great fisherman so picking his brain is always a good idea!

"So any fish tales today?" I asked.

"It's been pretty slow. I picked up one last night on the Breadline but I really don't know why...didn't mark any bait up there," he replied.

"Well since I don't have a deckhand today...they are still in school...I think I will head up there too. It's a nice straight drag. I can point the boat straight and set my gear. It's the first trip of the year and I'm tellin' ya fish are gonna die!" I said.

Ben laughed and said, "Go get 'em there tiger!"

I laughed and went on my merry way.

Got the boat ready, baited up the gear and fired up the motors to warm them up when my phone rang. It was my people for the day...they were at the top of the dock thirty minutes early! Crap I hate it when they do that! So I started to run up the dock to get them and had to stop about half way to catch my breath...I forgot that I was not in boat shape yet! Damn near passed out! Caught my breath and took a more leisurely stroll on up the dock.

Funny thing is I really never know what to expect when I meet my guests each day. They book the trip either online or over the phone. They have seen my pics online but I have no idea what they look like. Sometimes they look like you envisioned and other times not so much. This family booked via email...no conversations...no clues other than the last name Potenze and the fact that they were from New Jersey. So of course I imagined them to look like the mob. Pinstriped suits...slicked black hair...wingtip shoes...tired serious nervous look...Good Fellas all the way. And when I got to the top of the dock I found a family of four...two kids with wild long black hair in parkas like it was forty below and a blonde headed mom named Traci that sounded like the Jersey Shore. When she opened her mouth the most nasally scratchy sound came out...worse than fingernails on a blackboard! I instantly thought...it's gonna be a long 4 hours! She wore yoga pants that left little to the imagination and had on earmuffs and the most gaudy tacky floral print jacket I had ever seen! Dad, JD did in fact have on black wingtips but no suit just perfectly creased jeans and a button down shirt with monograms and rings on every finger. The kids were about ten and twelve and in need of a damn good thrashing! Loud and obnoxious but not in an endearing way...more like two spoiled brats! They were Tina and Junior...Tina looked a lot like mom or at least she tried to and Junior looked like a fat little Xbox boy! You know the kind that sit around drinking sixty-four ounce sodas, eating Skittles and chips all day playing Call of Duty!

"Great...fishing with the mob! Better catch something...wouldn't want to end up sleepin' with the fishes!" I thought.

Once we got on the boat things started to settle down...I did my usual safety briefing and they laughed at all my old jokes right on cue and we headed out to the fishing grounds. On the way I asked everyone what they did for a living...like I always do...and they replied.

"I'm in business security."

"We go to school."

"I'm a stay at home mom." To which I replied, "So you are the one with the REAL job!" They all laughed.

We got to the grounds and I put the gear in the water. Just as I set the last rod in the holder it popped out of the downrigger and the reel started screaming! I quickly handed it off to Traci and she started laughing and screaming all at the same time. I coached her through the catching, she was awful by the way but somehow we managed to land a beautiful twenty-two pound king!

It ran on her three times...as they usually do and every time she would squeal that nasally otherworldly screech and laugh and laugh! She was killin' me but I have to admit it was a ton of fun!

Once the beast was in the net I went into cruise control...I flipped it onto the deck...measured it to make sure it was legal even though I knew it was...and I grabbed the trusty Louisville Slugger and whacked it on the head with a loud satisfying thunk!

Mom screamed again, "What the hell are you doing! Why did you do that?"

"To put it out of its misery. It's what we do!" I said.

"Oh my god! That was so barbaric! You

are traumatizing my children!" she said.

"Honey…that's were food comes from!" I said.

JD started laughing, "Honey he is right…besides it's no worse than those damn games the kids play all the freakin' time!"

Then one of the kids said under his breath, "Besides that's kinda what you do for a living isn't it dad?"

All the laughter suddenly stopped. JD looked around the boat and said, "Son we are on vacation…no shop talk up here."

The mood had changed so fast and become so heavy it was crushing the very breath out of my lungs and I was desperately trying to find a way out when another fish hit the rod that was still in the water on the port side of the boat!

And just as quickly we were back in happy vacationland and I was completely relieved!

Junior grabbed the rod this time and fought the fish like he had fished for salmon his whole life. It was so good to watch! The fish ran only twice and I missed it on the first try with the net...it was the first trip after all so I was a little out of practice! But I got it the second try and when the fish hit the deck Junior announced, "Can I whack the fish? Can I?"

JD just shook his head and laughed and I said, "Sure! Whack away!"

He then proceeded to beat the living crap out of that poor fish! Even mom seemed okay with it this time.

I put the gear down and we trolled for about another hour without a bite. I told jokes and stories about Alaska and everyone had a great time. It was time to head in so I pulled the gear and we headed for home.

When we got back Ben was waiting to hassle me. He asked, "Well...did any fish die?"

I opened up the fish box and proudly flipped both kings on the deck and said, "I've got a pair of kings…what do you have?"

He said "Damn! That's what I'm talkin' about! Good job!"

I thanked everyone for the business and JD said "You know…this was the highlight of our vacation! Thank you so much…I'm afraid I have run out of cash so I can't give you a tip today. You will get your tip in a few days after we get home. Thanks again."

I told him "No worries! I'm just glad you had a good time and that we caught some fish!" Of course I was privately thinking, "You cheap bastard! Yeah I'll never hear from you again!"

They went up the dock and Ben came back over and I told him about the tip is in the mail thing and we both had a good laugh!

The first trip of the year was a complete success! Fish on!

The Tip

A couple of weeks had passed and the first trip of the season was now a distant memory. The fishing was typical May fishing...a king here and a king there but no consistency to speak of. When the fishing is slow like it almost always is in May those four hour trips seem like eight hour trips and the six and eight hour trips are simply excruciating! You get to do the old song and dance routine... telling stories and jokes and lies...the same stories and jokes and lies over and over again! Tap dancing on the back deck gets old but it's all part of the game. When the fish do finally show up in numbers all the captains collective moods are elevated! Hell we almost become giddy!

Anyway I had just finished one of those painfully long days of fishing uninterrupted by catching and had cleaned up the boat...which didn't take long as there were no fish that day. Speaking of cleaning up the boat...I could not wait...it was only one more week and my deckhands would be out of school and they would have to clean the boat! Yes! But once again I digress.

As I was walking up the dock to head to the house Cindy called.

"Hey! What's up?" I answered.

"Did you catch anything today?" she asked.

"Na...the fishing was good but the catching sucked! It's May."

"Hey I got a strange call today from the bank...they said that the boat loan had been paid off and they wanted to know if we wanted all the documents mailed to us or if we just wanted to swing by and pick them up? Do you know anything about this?" she queried.

"That's gotta be a mistake. I certainly didn't just shit $60 grand to pay it off."

"That's what I thought too. I'll take an hour tomorrow and go see what has happened...they will probably figure out the error by then anyway! What do you say we go out to dinner and celebrate while we do own the boat even if it is just for a day!" she laughed.

"Sounds good to me! I'll be home in about fifteen!" I said.

When I got home she was waiting in the driveway ready to go. We had a nice dinner and toasted our fake accomplishment and had a good laugh!

The next morning I got down to the boat about 7 a.m....my trip was at 8:30 a.m....thought I would get some new leaders tied that morning. When I got there I found a large manila envelope laying on one of the seats of the boat. I looked at it and laughed "What has Ben done now?"

You see we captains are always playing tricks on each other...hiding bananas on boats, leaving crazy notes, just your average everyday twelve year old boy kinda mischief.

Just as I sat down and started to reach for the mystery envelope my phone rang. "Blocked number" is all the caller id said..."Hmmm what is this?" I thought.

I answered the phone, "Lost in Alaska Adventures, how may I help you?"

"Capt. Kevin...it's JD! Do you remember me?" said the caller in flashback inducing tone filled with a serious Jersey accent.

"Yeah, I remember you! We fished a few weeks ago and caught two kings! How are you?" I asked thinking he was calling to book another trip.

"Yes, that is right! Junior won't stop

taking about that trip. You treated us like family and we really had a great time! Did you happen to get that tip I promised you?" he asked.

"Uh...no sir. Haven't seen anything come in the mail."

"The bank did not call you yesterday?" he asked.

I instantly was filled with a combination of dread and confusion. I tried to collect my thoughts and act like The Fonz...be cool! "Yeah the bank did call my wife and told her the note had been paid off...we thought it was a mistake! That was your doing?"

"Oh good they did call. I told them to do that...you see you treated us like family and now we are treating you like family!" he announced in an ominously cheerful tone.

"JD...that is really too much! We really can't accept that kind of a gesture. It's very kind...too kind in fact! We are just a small little charter company and it's just too much! I will call the bank and tell them to reverse the funds immediately."

He then said, "I thought you might say something like that so I instructed the bank not to allow that...this transaction is a done deal. You are now part of our family and we take care of our own!"

"But...," I tried to interject but was quickly interrupted.

"Capt. Kevin...it's not open to discussion! We have now helped you and one day we will ask you for a favor in return and since you are now family you will help us out...understand?" With that his tone became much more serious.

He continued, "We know all about your little charter business. We know you are not going to get rich fishing and we even know that you captains all say it's a lifestyle choice...we get that. But we have decided to take you under our wing...and make sure your little business is just a little more profitable. Do you remember asking what I did for a living? I said I work in business security…that's my business' security and your business' security. You help me secure my business and I help you secure your business…it's all good. You will see."

"I don't think I want to be involved in this business…I don't like this at all!" I protested.

"Let me try to convince you that doing business with us is both profitable and necessary for your business. Just hear me out okay?" His tone once again changed and he sounded like every telemarketer that has ever been!

"I'm really not interested! I'm calling the bank and this is over!" I shouted.

The smooth telemarketer started back up, "Capt. Kevin…hear me out. You really are in need of our services and here is why…there is an envelope on the seat in front of you…please pick it up but don't open it just yet. You see we know exactly how much money you make a year…don't ask how…just know that we do. We want to help you make even more! Doesn't that sound good? More money is always a good thing! I'm just going to cut to the chase...part of my job in business security is to solve problems...or should I say make problems go away...forever! But we have a different style, a certain je ne sais quoi if you will. When a problem needs to go away forever we like to send them on an all-expense paid vacation...but not just any vacation...a true trip of a lifetime! After fishing with you we know that you can and will provide the perfect experience for our guests. And since we do know everything about your business we know that you must be compensated appropriately so every charter we book with you we will pay your normal full fare and we will tip you $100,000 cash in unmarked bills...oh and your deckhand will receive a $50,000 tip as well! And all you have to do is take our guests out and show them the absolute best time you can and then at the end of the trip...right after they tell you how great the trip was and we know that they will...then you must kill them and dispose of their bodies! We know this is in your skill set...you see I remember you telling us all about Lynn Canal and how it was 2600 feet deep and then joking, 'That's where we hide the bodies!' You see...we know everything about your business!"

I exclaimed, "There is no way! I'm not a murderer! This is not happening!"

He calmly continued, "Capt. Kevin would you go ahead and open that envelope...in it you will find all the inspiration you will need to enter into this business relationship. The first picture...she sure is a sweet looking little old lady...isn't her ringtone on your phone *The Little Old Lady from Pasadena*? And the second picture is your lovely wife and I believe her ringtone is *Cherry Pie* is it not? And the next picture would be your two lovely nieces Sara and Jamie...and their ringtones are *Hey Hey We're The Monkees* and the theme to the *Munsters* TV shows. You really would not want any of these lovely ladies to fall into harm's way would you? Oh and the next picture is of your deckhand Merik's family...gotta have a little help from your friend. Now to be fair I'm going to let you think about our business offer for thirty seconds...if you still are not interested I will hit send on the group text that I just typed and all of these lovely ladies will be eliminated in the next five minutes! We don't mess around when it comes to business! And to prove that what I am telling you is true your niece Sara is about to text you a little message. Your time starts now!"

And with that he started humming the theme to Jeopardy!

At that very moment I did in fact receive a text from Sara that read "Hey Unkie...I'm talking to a guy that says he fished with you last summer! How cool is that?!"

I had no choice...so I agreed to do his bidding. I simply could not take a chance with their lives.

He then said, "I knew you would come

around. You will hear from me one day soon when I have a booking for you! Welcome to the family, Capt. Kevin!" and he hung up the phone.

The Talk

My trips that day were painfully long not due to a lack of fish action, but due to me trying to figure out exactly what I was into and how to possibly get out of it!

I was so glad to finally get home and see Cindy and Moose and have that first beer of the evening.

Cindy asked, "You seem a little on edge this evening?"

"Yeah a little...long day. Tomorrow you can go ahead and pick up that paperwork from the bank if you like," I said.

"What do you mean? I thought it was some kind of mistake," she said.

"Well...not exactly. I got a call today...do you remember that dick I took out from New Jersey that said he didn't have any cash for a tip...the one that said he would send the tip later...well he actually did send the tip! He called the bank and paid off the boat," I said.

"What! That is crazy!" she exclaimed.

"I know...I told him it was too much but he insisted. He also said he was going to send us a ton of business."

"That is great news! Do I need to call Brian and ask what that will do to our taxes?" she asked.

"Yeah that is a good idea. I'm sure it's gonna do a real number on us in the end! But we will make it work out," I said knowing full well that if we did one job for JD we would have plenty of money to offset our new tax burden.

I decided it was best not to tell Cindy any more info about what would be required of me on these new bookings. Besides I didn't know how to describe our new exclusive service… "Lost in Alaska Adventures…our customers love us to death!" Anyway I downed a few more beers and passed out as I hit the pillow.

The next morning was Merik's first day back on the boat. School was finally out and my deckhands were back! This fact excited me quite a bit until he told me "Yesterday morning Dad got stopped at Breeze Inn by a dude that said he had gone fishing with us…you really do know everyone in town I guess!"

I laughed nervously "Yeah I suppose I do…hey let's get ready for the trip and if you don't mind when the trip is over I'd like to head back out for an hour or two and see if we can catch a king for our freezer!"

"Sweet! I'm down with that!" he replied.

I wanted to go back out so we could talk privately about our new situation. How the hell was I going to tell him he was going to have to help me kill people and get rid of their bodies. It's not like I could say, "Merik...we have a new trip this year...a four hour Sleeps with the Fishes tour! Not only do you get to club the salmon...you get to club the customers!"

Oh well...we will deal with that later I suppose. We loaded up our guests and went out for a nice four hour salmon trip and it was good to see Merik running the back deck again. Merik has been working for me for many years...got to watch him grow up and it has been amazing to see. He's a good lookin' young guy with dark hair, a good easy going attitude, and a smile that all the young girls and the old girls for that matter seem to fall for! It is fun to watch him squirm when a seventy year old cougar tries to take him back to her stateroom on the cruise ship! Good times indeed!

We had two folks on board and we managed to catch a couple of nice kings and they were very happy! Once we were back at the dock and had the fish dealt with he did a quick clean on the boat and we headed back out to do a little fishing and a lot of talking.

Merik put the gear down and we started trolling on the backside of Douglas Island…might as well try there since we had done so well there earlier.

"Well here goes…" I thought and continued out loud, "Merik…we have to talk about something. It's really serious and totally sucks and I really don't know any other way of telling you so I'm just gonna say what I have to say."

"Okay…what is up?" he asked.

"That man that talked to your dad yesterday morning…he's a real bad dude. He was going to kill your dad if I didn't agree to do some really bad things," I said.

"What! What are you talking about!" he asked in a very scared way!

"Please just hear me out…that guy that I texted you about that said he didn't have any cash and he said he would send the tip later...well he did. He paid off my boat and is now blackmailing me into doing some horrible things! And these things involve you too. Apparently he is in the mob and if we don't do as he says he will kill Cindy, my mom, our nieces, and everyone in your family too. He had one of his goons go up to my niece Sara and pretend to have gone fishing with us just as we were talking...just like the man that came up to your dad...and Sara sent me a text about the conversation as I was having to decide if I was going to go along with his offer."

Just then I received a text that read "Show this to Merik...Hello Merik...you don't know me but am looking at your sisters right now! Sure would be a shame..."

Merik freaked out...understandably as did I! How did they know we were having this conversation....the damn boat must be bugged!

After about an hour I got him to calm down a bit and I told him the rest of the story. Everything...how much he was going to be paid...how we had to play it like it was a normal charter...everything! I told him I would do the actual killing... he just had to help me sink the bodies. I also assured him that somehow some way I would come up with a way to get us out of this mess. I also told him he could never tell anyone or everyone would be killed. He ultimately agreed to help me. I watched him age a good ten years that evening and I really hated all of this stupidity!

We pulled the gear and headed for the dock. It was well over a week before we started to joke around again and I was so relieved when that finally happened.

Then I got the call.

The Phone Rings

I was driving home after a long ten hour day on the water when JD called for the first trip. When the phone rang I looked down to see what the caller id read and it said "Blocked" and I hoped that it was just another telemarketer or political survey! It's pretty bad when you long for those type calls! So I answered it and alas it was dickhead himself...JD!

"Hope you had a great day on the water there Captain!" he said.

"It was good until I heard your voice!"

"Now, now...I'm calling with business so

it's all good! You need to pull over so you can write down all the info...I'll wait for you," he said.

"How the hell does he always know exactly what I'm doing and where I am?" I thought and I replied, "Pulling over now."

"Are you available for a four hour salmon trip on June 21st at 5pm?" he asked.

"Nope, I'm full that day!" I gladly said lying through my teeth.

"Ha nice try! I know you are lying! Your trip will be at 5 p.m....I figured night time was the best time for these trips...wouldn't you agree?" he said with smile in his voice.

"Doesn't really matter as that is Summer Solstice and the sun won't really go down until almost midnight. Besides Monday mornings may be better as there are no cruise ships in until 11 a.m. so the water is a lot less crowed," I said.

"Good to know...but of course you realize I already knew that!" he laughed and continued. "Your guests will be at your dock at 5 p.m. The name is Sam Barnes and his wife Jane and it will be just the two of them."

"I've been meaning to ask...how the hell am I supposed to do this? This is completely outside of my wheelhouse! I'm still not sure I can do this!" I said.

"You can do it! If it helps Sam is not a very good guy...we caught him skimming off our deposits and he killed two of our best men...," he said.

I interrupted, "Stop! I don't want to know anything! I'm assuming that they are all bad people!"

He laughed "That's a good assumption! And just so you know on the evening of the 20th you will find a special gift in the back of your truck and that special gift would be perfect for these little trips. You are welcome!"

"Wow! You really do think of everything don't you...Dick!"

"Ha ha...have a good trip and you will

find two envelopes on the seat of your truck when you get back. Don't spend it all in one place! And you could try to be a little more respectful towards me you know!" as he hung up laughing.

I threw down my phone in disgust and thought, "Wow! I guess it's really gonna happen! I'm gonna be a fucking Soprano! A Good Fella! A Reservoir Dog! Make that a Lynn Canal Dog! Fuck me!"

The First Job

On my way to the boat I stopped and picked up a couple of cinder blocks and some good rope to help with the disposal...try to sink them if I could. Was not at all sure if that would even work but hoped it did. And the night before just like clockwork there was indeed a special gift placed in the back of my truck...a 9mm Smith & Wesson with an Iron Ridge suppressor and six boxes of ammo. The suppressor really threw the balance off on the weapon and I quickly decided I would have to use two hands to have any chance of hitting a target with the damn thing. Still had huge doubts as to whether I would be able to pull this off.

I waited to tell Merik about the first job until right before the trip. I knew he would be completely freaked and I thought it might help if he didn't have to think about it…if he could just react to it.

Well, I loaded up the boat with all this lovely new gear and waited for Merik to get there…had to stay cool as we had an eight hour halibut & salmon combo trip to get through first.

He got there and I tried to joke a bit but I guess I was not as cool as I had hoped. He soon asked if something was bothering me and I laughed and shook my head. This seemed to satisfy him for the time being.

Our guests showed up and we went out and limited on halibut in less than an hour and then trolled for salmon for a few hours…catching six Chum salmon that we released as they only wanted Kings or Coho. All in all it was a good trip but it must have been obvious that I was not on my game because as soon as the people were gone and the catch was processed, Merik sat down across from me and asked, "Okay...what is going on?"

"Merik...our first job is tonight. The Barnes group at 5 p.m. is a one way trip."

All the color drained from his face and he quickly ran to the back deck, leaned over the side and threw up.

"We have to play it really cool. Just like any other trip. Joke with them tell them stories...just be you. I will do the deed...follow my lead. We will get through this together," I said.

"Okay...I'll try," he replied.

"If it helps any JD said that Mr. Barnes is really a bad dude."

About that same time Merik got a text from his dad about how he just met a guy that had been on the boat. He showed it to me and I said, "Bastards!"

I told him to get the boat ready and I headed up the dock to meet the Barnes.

When I got to the top of the dock the taxi was just pulling in and it was showtime.

They got out of the taxi and I introduced myself and shook hands with Mr. Barnes and his wife. I was really glad that she was not a hugger!

He looked to be in his mid-50's. He had salt and pepper hair and a very nervous smile…the kind of smile that looks very forced at best. Other than that smile he did not look like a horrible person.

It was obvious that his wife really did not want to be there…she was wearing a white pants suit which is not ideal for a fishing trip and her hair was big and "done" like she had just left the local beauty salon after sitting under a hair dryer from the 50's for several hours! And she smelled like Chanel…lots of Chanel…as if she was trying to cover up the fact that she had not bathed for several days so she would not mess up her hair! I could not help but wonder if she was personally responsible for that hole in the ozone layer! The amount of hairspray present made her hair look like a helmet...it might even be bullet proof! That could be a real problem!

On the way down the dock she complained, "This place is completely uncivilized...how can you live without a Saks? It's rained here every day since we got here! It's just so depressing! Why would anyone want to live here? I'll never understand!"

I kind of laughed and told her, "Yes it rains here a lot...it is a rainforest after all. And it is true that we don't have a Saks but we do have a Fred Meyers!"

She gave me a go to hell look and her husband snickered just a bit.

We loaded up and I noticed that Merik was doing his best to stay cool and we headed out for the fishing grounds. I had heard from Capt. Ben that he had found a few more fish out in the False Pt. Retreat area so we headed there...this worked well as I had planned to do the deed in Barlow Cove...thought it would be nice and quiet in there...no other boats.

We ran about thirty-five minutes and Merik put the gear down and we started fishing. The fishing was not what I had hoped for...all we could find were shaker kings! Too small to keep...not that they were going to keep any fish that night!

She continued to rail on about this god forsaken place! And how their hotel sucked and how her husband wouldn't listen to her and how she really didn't like my beard!

Mr. Barnes asked her to shut the hell up and all hell broke loose! They started screaming at each other and calling each other names I had never heard before and that says something...I'm a freakin' sailor!

They cussed each other for a good hour...all the time I kept on trolling around Pt. Retreat and into Barlow Cove.

As we passed the Pt. Retreat Lighthouse

I tried to point out how beautiful it was and she said, "I don't care about your fucking ugly ass lighthouse! Fuck it and fuck this place!" He went off on her again.

I quietly thought, "Wow! They are making this a lot easier! Does that make me a bad person?" I answered myself, "Yeah, it does."

I looked all around and was very pleased to find that Barlow was completely empty...no boats anywhere. I reached into my trusty red bag...the one I carry all of my important documents in everyday and quietly pulled out the Smith & Wesson and took the safety off. I walked to the back deck...they were still screaming at each other and I shouted, "Enough!"

They both snapped their heads around and looked at me with a look that screamed, "How dare you!"

I quickly and effortlessly raised the gun and aimed at her head and pulled the trigger! I then whipped the gun around on him and said, "That was a favor! You are welcome!" and pulled the trigger again!

Somehow she had managed to fall straight back on to the deck and he almost fell out of the boat but instinctively Merik had grabbed him to keep him from falling overboard.

"Merik, we have work to do!" I continued, "You pull the gear and I'll get them ready!"

He nodded and went to work. Having him just react instead of telling him in advance was proving to be a great idea I decided.

I quickly pulled out the four cinder blocks I had brought down to the boat and tied their two bodies together at the waist and then tied the remaining eight foot piece of rope to the cinder blocks.

I looked at the depth sounder and saw that we had drifted to about 500 feet of water and I asked Merik to help me pick up and then lower the bodies into the water. I really hoped the cinderblocks would be enough to start them down. Once the bodies were in the water we grabbed the cinder blocks and lowered them into the water too and I glanced up again at the depth sounder and it read 600 feet now and I said, "Here goes!" And we released the weight. I was so relieved that they started straight down...no hesitation...and they were going down very fast.

"Let's head to the barn," I said. "We really have to do a good clean tonight!"

He said, "I'll start now."

I was a bit surprised...it was not as messy as I thought it would be...but then again we do tend to cover the back deck in blood on a regular basis.

When we got back to the dock we finished cleaning the boat and fueled up for the next day.

When we got to the top of the dock I opened my truck door and sitting on the seat were two envelopes. I handed Merik his...he took it and asked, "7:30 a.m. tomorrow?"

"Yep...see you then. Try to get some sleep," I answered and he walked to his car.

A Few Good Days

We did not speak of the first job for several days. We just showed up for work and put on our game faces and worked like everything was normal. I was actually quite impressed with the poise Merik was showing in these dire circumstances...remember he is only eighteen years old. I was truly wishing at that point that I had never hired a deckhand...that I had not put him in this situation. But alas, it is what it is.

In between trips on the third day he finally broke the silence, "Kevin...I really didn't think you could to that. I mean it was so out of character for you. You laugh and joke and kid people…you don't kill them! How the hell did you do it?"

"Well, I didn't think I could either. But I thought about all the people that I love that would be hurt if I didn't…and I thought about your family…and I thought about how these people are really bad people to start with, I mean you saw how they raised hell with me and each other the whole time, they really were awful people…and then I thought again about my family…"

"But how did you do it? I don't think I could have!" he asked.

"I got so angry with the fact that I had no choice…I just got angry. Then I had an idea…I would just pretend I was playing a video game…you know like Assassin's Creed and I went there! It was all I could do. And now here we are," I said.

"Do you think we are done? I really hope so!" he asked.

"I hope so but I don't think we are. We won't be done until we figure out a way to kill JD!"

"I've thought about it a lot and if you do get another job...let's do it like last time...don't tell me until right before the trip...it's best that way," he said.

"Deal! I think it is best if you just react instead of worry. Now let's go catch some fish!"

We went out that afternoon and destroyed the salmon and we both seemed a little more like ourselves.

In the truck on the way home, JD called with another job.

"Captain, I have another trip for you. It's this Monday morning...didn't you say Monday mornings were a good time for these trips?"

"Yes, I did. 8 a.m. good for you?" I asked.

"Ah you read my mind. The name is Wilson and it will be two brothers this time. And they really want halibut...

remember this is a Bucket List trip!" he laughed.

"Yeah, I got it. Whatever!" I said.

"I know you don't want to know anything about our guests but I'm going to tell you anyway! These boys made their living ripping off little old ladies...like your mom! Selling them security systems...protection if you will...and that is our racket! They scammed the boss' mom and now they are coming to see you! Have fun with that!" he said.

"Lovely...always scum of the earth! Maybe you should find some better friends!" I laughed.

"Maybe so...don't piss me off! And just a heads up...I may be needing a whole week of trips in a few weeks...we will see. Talk to you soon!" and he hung up the phone.

"Well, I guess I'll have to get more supplies...Crap!" I thought.

The New Halibut Hole

The forecast was not exactly friendly for our Monday morning trip. In fact, it was calling for thirty knot winds out of the south and quite rough seas. Normally I would have cancelled the trip but this being a special one way trip that was not an option.

We discussed the alternatives and decided the only place we might be able to go was Barlow Cove...there we could hide from the wind and sea. We've caught halibut in there but it is usually really slow fishing. Oh well...if these boys didn't catch anything I was not gonna worry about it. It's not like they were gonna go on TripAdvisor afterwards.

It was raining sideways...kinda normal for Juneau...and I was waiting at the top of the dock in my rain gear when the Wilson boys arrived.

They got out of the taxi and they were both wearing t-shirts, shorts, flip flops, and light windbreakers! So I asked, "You guys know we are going fishing in Alaska?"

Pete was the first to speak, "Ha...this is how we fish! We are on vacation and this is what we do!"

"Okay...could be a long four hours! Good thing I brought coffee!" I said.

Pete looks mid 40's and about 5' 8" and maybe 160 pounds soaking wet...and he would be just that today!

Tom looked a little younger and was

about the same size. They both had George Hamiltonesque tans...and teeth so white they glowed! I thought, "Yeah I could see these boys charming the knickers off of little old ladies. Bastards!"

As we were leaving the harbor I told them that it could get a little bumpy and they both looked at me and smiled those freakishly glowing white teeth at me and Tom said, "Bring it! We have been waiting for this our entire lives!"

Working our way across to South Shelter was fun to say the least! Solid 3 foot seas with the occasional 4 footer! But we were pounding into it so coming home would not be too bad.

Once we rounded the spit at South Shelter the water got a lot better! On the way to Barlow I glassed up past Pt. Retreat and it looked really nasty! "Merik...I see a lot of sheep in the field! We are gonna stay in Barlow today!"

"Sounds good to me...I'll get the gear ready!" he replied.

We pulled into Barlow and there was a little chop but it was certainly fishable.

"I hope we don't snag those other bodies!" I privately thought and I told Merik to send the gear down.

This was a genuine concerns as we were less than 100 yards from where we had laid them to rest.

Much to my surprise when the bait hit bottom the boys almost instantly had bites! Within thirty seconds we had two fish on! The way they were fighting they were definitely halibut!

The boys got them to the surface and decided to go for bigger fish so we released them and back down they went! Once again as soon as they hit bottom…two more on the line! They continued to repeat this same action for about an hour then Pete said, "I'm frickin' freezin'…I gotta warm up!" and he did come on in for a few minutes.

Tom on the other hand was a machine! He was shivering and turning blue but was having way too much fun to stop.

After about ten minutes Pete rejoined his brother and they kept reeling fish up for about another thirty minutes. I could tell they were getting tired so I decided it was time to do the deed.

I went into the cabin and once again pulled out the Smith & Wesson, took the safety off and walked back to the back deck. I gave Merik a look and then I pointed the gun at the back of Tom's head as he was bringing up another fish. I pulled the trigger and the damn thing jammed!

They both instantly turned towards me and screamed, "What the fuck is this?"

They dropped their rods and came at me. Merik grabbed Pete and began wrestling with him. I threw the gun into the cabin and started fighting off Tom.

Merik managed to get Pete up against the door of the head and had him fairly well under control.

Tom and I were rolling on the floor when

I saw the mini Louisville Slugger we use for bonking fish on the head. I grabbed it, turned and swung like I was going for the fence!

It hit him right square in the forehead and dazed him just long enough for me to deliver six or seven…I lost count…more solid blows to his head and face. He went limp and rolled over on the deck.

I then jumped up and went to town on Pete while Merik tried to hold him still. After a few more good blows to the old noggin Pete went down!

I told Merik, "Just throw the rods overboard and help me tie these guys up!"

He said, "The rods are gone! The fish they had on took them while we were fighting!"

"Shit! Well, here's a rope! Tie Pete up!" I yelled.

We managed to get them tied up together and tied the cinder blocks down by their feet and we picked them up and threw them overboard. We then threw the cinder blocks over and they started spiraling down. After about twenty seconds we saw air bubbles rise to the surface.

On the way back in...after Merik had cleaned up the deck...I told him, "Thanks for the help there! That really sucked donkey dicks!"

"No shit!" he replied.

"I'll make damn sure that doesn't happen again. Oh and we are so done for the day! I'm cancelling the afternoon trip," I said.

"Thank you!" he said and we made our way to the dock and went home.

Planning Ahead

The next morning our trip did not start until noon so I took advantage of that precious spare time to try to put some sort of a plan in place...even if it was futile I had to try.

I went to Fred Meyer and bought a TracFone and a few minutes so I could have a phone that JD did not know about...at least for a few minutes. And I called my old friend Dan Berg in Tulsa.

Dan and I have been friends for over thirty years so I knew I could count on him. He is a mountain of a man...6'6" and full of laughter and good stories. He and I played in a band back in the day...back when we both had hair! And we worked in radio together. He is an overall good man.

I called him and even though he was at work he answered...I'm guessing he thought I was a business call.

"Dan...I know you are at work but dude I've really got to talk to you. Can you give me five minutes?" I asked.

"Kevy! Didn't recognize the number! I'm driving to a meeting so now is perfect! What's up?" he said.

"Great! Listen I can't tell you all of the particulars but I have gotten myself into some really heavy shit! There's a lot of crazy things that could come to pass...that's why I called on a strange phone...pretty sure mine has been bugged," I said.

He interrupted, "Dude...is it the government? What have you done?"

"No it's not that…that would be a dream compared to what I'm dealing with! I really can't tell you anything at this time. If all goes well maybe one day we can laugh about it over a beer! But right now it's really serious and I can't talk long so hear me out and please do what I ask."

"You got it! I'm all ears!" he said.

"Okay…if I need you to act I will send you a text that reads Mom Disappear! If you get that text no matter where you are or what you are doing or what time it is you must drop everything and go to my mom's house and make her disappear! It could be really dangerous and I'm sorry to ask you to possibly put yourself in harm's way but I may not have a choice I'm dealing with some really bad people here and they mean business. I will make sure she knows to go with you. When it is safe I will let you know."

"You know I'll do it! No worries! Just wish I knew more," he replied.

"And if Cindy is travelling for work and is

anywhere near you I may send Cindy Disappear and the name of the city she is in. If I could tell you more I would but honestly I may have already told you too much! Thank you my brother! I'll be in touch!" I said.

"Love you too, Bro...I'm here any time!" and we both hung up.

I then called Jamie's husband Adam and set up the same arrangement for her and Sara.

Really didn't know if it would work but I had to try something. Surprisingly it did give me a little piece of mind.

When I got to the boat I recommended to Merik that he might want to do the same thing and he agreed to do just that.

We went out on the water and actually had a good fishing trip...the fishing was good and we both had a little piece of mind...any plan was better than no plan!

Three Times The Fun

Did not hear from JD for a whole week! Best damn week of the season so far!

Phone rings. "I was wondering what happened to you," I said.

"Ha…been a little busy. Had to deal with some things so you didn't have to! Do you remember I said I may need you to do whole week of trips coming up?" he asked.

"Yeah I remember that…when and who?" I asked knowing that arguing with him was not going to help.

"Slow down there...there were going to be five but like I said I personally had to deal with one of them...it got stupid and he had to go! And another guy had a heart attack so mother nature took care of that problem so I only have three for you and it will be next Monday and Tuesday," he said.

"Wait a minute! Three in two days is way too much! How the hell am I supposed to do that?" I complained.

"No worries there Captain...I've got it all figured out! Monday morning you will take Billy Franks and his son fishing and once the deed is done you will proceed to Hoonah to pick up Jim Carr and his lovely wife who will have just completed a bear viewing tour and you will fish on the way back to Juneau. Then Tuesday morning you get to take Marvin Jones and his lovely bride out to see the whales...no fishing this time," he said as if he were very proud of the way he had worked it all out.

"That will all be fine if the water cooperates...if it kicks up and I can't get to Hoonah what then Mister Know-it-all?" I asked.

"Well, Captain Jackass…if that happens we will fly the Carrs back to Juneau and you will get them Tuesday! So there!" he snapped.

"Well I guess you do have it all figured out! Thanks for ruining my week!" I shouted.

He laughed, "Glad I could be of service! Have a great week!" and he hung up.

Busy Couple Of Days

On my way to the boat on Monday morning I stopped at Home Depot to pick up all the supplies we were going to need for the next three trips. I grabbed a cart and made my way to the rope section and found a nice 200' braided rope and threw it in the cart. Then I made my way to the cinder block section and I started to load those suckers on the cart. While I was loading them a clerk came up and asked if I needed any help...and then proceeded to help with loading up the cart, "So how many do you need?" he asked.

"Twenty-four," I responded.

"So what are you building with these?" he asked.

"Oh I'm not building anything...I'm just using them to hide bodies!" I quipped.

"Ha...that's funny! No really...what are you working on?" he laughed.

"Just a foundation...that's all." I said thinking he really doesn't want to know.

"Very good...do you need some rebar too?" he asked.

"Na...I'm good...thanks!" I said.

"Okay! You have a great day!" and he walked away towards the plumbing section of the store.

I have to admit telling him the truth was quite cathartic. Maybe I should try that more often...and then again maybe not.

Anyway I paid for the stuff and loaded it in the truck and made my way to the dock.

Merik met me at the top of the dock and I told him to load sixteen of the blocks into the boat and he looked at me and nodded...he knew what that meant.

Being a Monday morning I was hoping not to run into to many folks on the dock...really didn't want to explain all the blocks but we got to anyway. Capt. Ben was down on his boat as we came by.

"What you doin' with all those blocks?" he asked.

"Oh, I got a call from a buddy in Hoonah that needs them so we are running over there this morning and it worked out just perfect as last night I had two people call about a water taxi over to Hoonah so now the trip is paid for!" I said.

"Nice! Just got a report from one of the lodge boats it is flat all the way! Have a good trip!" he said.

"Excellent! Are you fishing today?" I asked.

"Yeah...halibut trip. Going up north," he said.

"I killed the halibut a few days ago in Barlow...just sayin'!"

"Really? Well we just might try that!" he continued. "Thanks!"

"Anytime!" I said and turned to get the boat ready.

When Billy Franks and his son Nathan showed up they were quite eager to find some fish. They asked about all the cinder blocks and I told them that after their trip we had to run them out to a buddy's cabin on one of the islands...help a friend out.

Billy seemed like a likeable guy...60'ish with a clean shaved head and several tattoos on his arms and Nathan was mid 20's with long red hair and he too had a few tattoos.

We could tell right away that Nathan was the fisherman. It was easy...he told us so! He was also a raging conversationalist we would soon find out!

As we were leaving the harbor another captain...Capt. Chris Conder to be exact...called me on the radio with a fish report.

"Fished Lizard Head last night and it was really good! Lots of Coho and a few Kings! If you've got the time it's worth the run!" he said.

"Very cool," I replied. "Thanks for the heads up!"

Nathan then chimed in, "He's lying to you! I'm a fisherman and no fisherman ever tells another fisherman where to go! I know!"

I laughed, "Well...actually all of us captains work together and we do share information. He's telling the truth...that's the way we do it here."

"No way! He is lying! Why the hell would

he tell you the truth? If you go there we won't catch shit! I know it and I will be pissed!" he insisted.

"Nathan...we work together because the more people that catch fish the more people that come back! It's beneficial to all of us. And I was already going to Lizard Head before he gave me the update...that just confirmed my decision."

"You mark my words...he's lying and we are not gonna catch shit!" he insisted.

I just shook my head and laughed and Billy then chimed in, "Son...not all businesses are as cutthroat as ours. I learned long ago that you don't want to piss off your captain or he will make damn sure that you don't catch any fish! Am I right there, Captain?"

"Ha...very true!" I responded.

After a few minutes of silence Nathan decided to continue telling us how awesome fishing in the Atlantic is and how many fish he had caught and how he was thinking about becoming a professional fisherman.

His mouth never stopped for the entire hour and a half run to the fishing grounds. Billy leaned over, "He's just excited...he will calm down once we start fishing."

I nodded in agreement and pulled back on the throttle and said, "Merik...let's go get 'em! Time to fish!"

Nathan went on the back deck to watch every move Merik made. Oh and he asked every question known to man! He was Merik's problem now. Good riddance!

The fish report was right...as I knew it would be! Before Merik could even set the drag on the first rod he yelled, "Fish on!" and handed the rod to Nathan.

He fought the fish for a few minutes then we landed it and it was a beautiful Coho...close to fifteen pounds!

Merik then quickly tried to set the gear and once again before he could even get to the second rod we had a fish on. This time he went ahead and set the second rod while Billy was fighting his fish and another fish hit that rod…doubleheader!

After the sixth fish came into the boat I walked back and poked Nathan in the chest with my finger and said, "Yep, Capt. Chris was lying to us! He's a dirty bastard that way!"

Nathan laughed and said, "I guess things are different up here. In our business it's kill or be killed! We all hate each other!"

I thought, "This is really gonna suck…this is the first of these one way trips where I have actually liked the people."

The fishing stayed hot and they were quickly reaching their limit. I looked around and we were so far out there were no other boats around so I decided to do the deed just after they landed their limit.

Merik yelled, "Doubleheader!"

I pulled out the Smith & Wesson and walked back to the door of the cabin and waited.

Both fish got to the stern of the boat at the same time and Merik skillfully netted them one right after the other and I shot Nathan in the back of the head and turned to Billy just as he said, "JD, you fucking bastard!" and I shot him right in the face.

We did the now familiar routine of tying up the bodies and attaching the blocks and sending them to the bottom...this time we had drifted to about 1200'.

I told Merik, "Bag up all the fish...we will donate them to charity when we get back so something good comes of this trip. And clean up as we head to Hoonah."

He looked confused... "We are picking up the next trip in Hoonah. They have been bear viewing and we are taking them fishing."

"I kind of liked them," he said.

"Yeah, I know...I did too," I replied as I

fired up the mains and pointed the boat toward Hoonah.

It only took us about thirty-five minutes to get to Hoonah so we were just a little early. I asked Merik if he wanted to get some lunch but he said he really was not hungry…truth be told neither was I but it seemed like something to do.

Hoonah is a quaint little fishing town on Chichagof Island. Surrounded by good fishing and tons of brown bears! There are bears everywhere! It's very beautiful but lots of bears!

Jim Carr and his wife Carrie showed up on the dock about an hour later. Their bear tour guide had just dropped them off without any indication of who would be picking them up so they started to wander the dock. They passed the boat and I asked, "Are you looking for someone in particular?"

Jim said, "We don't know who we are looking for! Just some boat that is supposed to take us to Juneau."

"Are you the Carrs?" I asked.

"Yes we are!" he replied and I welcomed them onto the boat.

They both struck me as accountant types. They were very nervous and very uncomfortable with everything that was going on. It was obvious that they were both fish out of water! Not outdoors folks if you know what I mean!

As we pulled away from the dock I asked them what they did for a living and instead of the usual casual answer I expected Jim said, "Why do you want to know?"

"Just small talk…just like to get to know my guests a little as we will be spending a little time together…that's all," I responded.

Carrie said, "Jim is just a little high strung. We are CPA's and you might be able to tell we have never done anything like this before! We have never been to a place like Hoonah…it really freaked us out."

"This is the kind of place where a person could make another person disappear!" Jim added and continued, "Do you know JD?"

This really took me off guard, "Uh...no I can't say that I know any person named JD. Why?" I asked.

"JD didn't set this trip up with you? If he didn't then who did?" he asked.

"This was booked by a travel agent named Claire...we have worked with her for years," I said lying through my teeth.

Then he turned to Merik, "Do you know JD?"

"No, the only JD I know is Juneau Douglas High School...I just graduated from there," he said playing it as cool as could be.

Then Carrie said, "Jim...calm down. They don't know him...can we just try to enjoy this trip?"

"I'll try but you know how JD works...and this trip came out of the blue! I just don't like it but I will try," he said.

With that Merik got out the license books and handed them to each of them and Jim said, "No thank you...I don't want to fish. This trip is for Carrie. I hate fish! I hate the smell, the taste, how their eyes never blink...they just stare at you! Fish are creepy...no thanks!"

"Is it okay if I am the only one that fishes?" she asked.

"Sure that is fine. What did you want to fish for salmon or halibut?" I asked.

"Halibut would be great! My daddy and I used to go fishing all the time. He passed a few years ago but I promised him I would catch a fish in Alaska for him one day so here I am," she said.

"I think we can do just that," I said.

We headed to one of my old halibut spots there in Icy Straits and dropped a line down.

Carrie brought up a cod and then a nice

big Yellow Eye rockfish but she was not satisfied she really wanted a halibut so she sent the line back down again.

Jim started back up with the questions, "So how much is JD paying you for this trip?"

"I'm sorry but I don't know a JD. The travel agent will send me a check next week," I said.

"How long have you worked with JD?" he asked.

"Sir...I really don't...," I started.

"Leave him alone!" Carrie interrupted "He doesn't know JD!"

"But this is just like something JD would do! Send us out on a boat in the middle of nowhere and have us killed!" he insisted.

"Look...JD said everything was okay as long as we paid back the money and we did! We did that over a year ago! Calm down and try to enjoy!" she said.

"I just don't trust him!" he started but

was quickly interrupted by her reel taking off in her hands.

Sure enough she had hooked into what looked like a nice halibut. It was even taking a little line.

I was sure glad that fish had come on to change the subject...I wasn't sure how much longer I could keep lying to this poor guy.

She fought the fish for a good long time and finally got it to the surface and Merik helped her land it.

While the fight was distracting everyone I managed to sneak out that Smith & Wesson again and got ready.

Once the fish was in the boat I pulled out the 9mm and pointed it at Jim and said, "Unfortunately you were right!" and shot him. I then turned on Carrie and said, "I'm so sorry!" and pulled the trigger.

We performed the usual tasks and headed for home.

"There's got to be a way to get out of this!" I thought.

We did not even say a single word all the way back to the dock. An hour and a half of silence...it was actually kind of nice. "Just drive the boat," I thought.

We got to the dock and tied up the boat and made our way up the dock. I opened my truck and handed Merik his two envelopes and I said, "7:30 a.m." and he nodded.

Sleep was not easy that night...actually it never happened. I just kept tossing and turning trying to find a way out of this mess.

Anyway we got to the boat and got ready the next morning. Merik knew once again instantly when he saw the blocks on the deck what was instore for the day.

Marvin and Jane Jones were late...could not find them anywhere and I had no way of calling them or JD since I had no number for either one. I was really getting nervous...what would JD do if they were a no show?! I was really starting to freak out when my phone rang and the harbor master's office told me they were over at the public dock and could I come over there to pick them up. Big time relief!

You see in Auke Bay there are two docks...the public and the private dock and we usually pick up at the private dock as that is where our slip is located.

Anyway we made our way over and they were waiting right at the foot of the gangway for us. So we loaded them up and took off.

"Is it just going to be the two of us?" Marvin asked.

"Yep...all of our trips are private trips!" I replied.

"Perfect!" he said.

I asked all my usual questions and found out that they had just been married the day before out at the glacier and that they were leaving Juneau right after our trip because he had to get back to work.

"Just a quick trip...we will do a real honeymoon later," he said.

I knew that this trip would be a whole lot more difficult to pull off as there are always a ton of whale boats around each group of whales. Could be tricky to find a private place.

I glassed around and spotted a few whale boats up by south Shelter Island and took off for that area.

When we got there the animals were down on a dive but I knew they were there so I announced, "The whales are down right now...let's just drift here for a few and see if they come back up."

I took the boat out of gear and we started to drift away from Shelter Island...the other boats were positioned just ahead of us and I was guessing that the whales would come up about 150 yards off of our port.

Well I was a little off...one came up and

spouted about 30 yards off or our port and this completely caught Jane by surprise. She was sitting next to me at the bow of the boat and she jumped straight up and started screaming, "They're gonna fucking kill us! Run for your lives! Run for your lives!" and she ran as fast as she could for the stern of the boat!

Just as she got there that whale spouted again right next to the boat and she screamed once again, "They're gonna kill us! They're gonna kill us! Run! Run for your lives!"

By now we are all laughing so hard there were tears coming down everyone's cheeks.

I asked her, "Exactly where were you going to run to? You are in a boat!"

"I was going to get out of this boat!" she said.

"Well then you would have been in the water with the whales...is that what you wanted?" I laughed.

"Oh hell no!" she said.

Marvin then tried to calm her down but as soon as another whale surfaced it all started again! "They're gonna kill us! Run!"

Once again we were in tears! I suggested that maybe we should leave those animals and look for some other marine critters and they agreed.

Marvin asked if we could go someplace a lot more private. With no boats around.

This seemed a bit odd to me but since I already needed to find a place just like that I agreed and I pointed the boat for the backside of Douglas.

She finally started to calm down some but she was really acting strangely. Very nervous and wary...I think we really may have traumatized the poor girl.

Then he started asking a lot of questions, "How deep is the water here? How cold is it? How long would a person survive in this water?"

I answered his questions but it seemed odd for some reason...maybe it was the tone that he asked them in...I'm not sure.

He then pointed to an island and asked what it was called and I replied, "Scull Island."

"Cool. Can we go behind that island and stop for a while?" he asked

"Sure," I said and we headed there.

We stopped and they made their way to the back of the boat...and I heard a huge splash!

I jumped up and ran to the back and found Jane was in the water splashing about.

"What the hell happened? Merik throw her the life ring!" I shouted.

"Not so fast!" Marvin shouted, "Leave her in the water! I have a deal for you, Captain...help me get rid of her and I'll give you a cut of the $5 million dollar life insurance policy I have on her."

I said, "No way!" and lunged at him only to have him shove me backwards into the cabin.

He said, "Then I will kill all of you!" and I heard gunshots go off. I grabbed for my gun.

I jumped up and spun around and saw him standing just outside of the doorway pointing his gun at the water and I realized that he had just shot her! I opened fire and emptied the clip! Merik dove and grabbed his gun hand and somehow managed to stay out of the line of fire.

By the time he stopped moving Jane was already dead and just barely floating under the surface of the water. I grabbed the gaff, hooked her in the shoulder and pulled her up to the boat. We then proceeded to tie them up and get the blocks attached and send them down.

Merik announced, "Wow! That guy was a piece of shit! I'm actually glad you shot him!"

"Yeah, me too," I said.

"That's the last time we go backside...too close to town!" I thought.

I was really nervous that someone would have seen or heard that trip...way too many rounds went off. I suppose we will have to wait and see.

Getting To Me

That night I was really starting to grow weary of all of this stupidity. And I suppose it was really starting to show as Cindy asked me, "Are you okay? You seem a lot more tired than you usually do at this point in the season."

"Yeah, I'm fine...just been a lot of twelve hour days in a row. That's all," I replied.

"Well I'm just worried. Would you like a shoulder rub?" she asked.

"Always!" I responded. Her shoulder rubs were always amazing! She has hands of steel!

I let her rub me for about ten minutes and it actually did start to relieve the stress just a bit.

When she was done she got me a cold beer and a glass of wine for herself and she found her way to the couch. About half way through her glass of wine she fell asleep. This was normal...she works really hard and sleeps on the couch while I watch TV fairly regularly. It is quite funny to watch her reaction when she wakes herself up snoring. Too funny!

Anyway...while she slept I stared at her and thought, "That is why I keep doing this!"

Then I started reviewing all of the one way trips in my mind. I knew that these people were all really bad but still some of them I actually liked...could they all be that bad?

I thought about their faces...what they said...their reactions to what was happening and my tough guy shell started to crack. The guilt and the remorse washed over me like wave...a tsunami of pain. Just when I thought I could not feel any more low I remembered that this nightmare was not over…there were deeper depths to fall.

I then looked at Cindy again sleeping on the couch next to me with her beautiful gentle face and I remembered how much I truly do love her and how much she truly loves me…why I'll never know…and I started to come out of that deep dark well.

I thought, "Gonna have to go full on pirate until I can solve this problem! And I will solve this problem…I will! We pirates are never more dangerous than when we are backed into a corner!"

With that I finished my beer and a couple of more before Cindy woke herself snoring again and we went to bed.

Facetime

The next day was a whole lot easier...just had two whale watching trips so I let Merik have the day off. He was thrilled!

Whale watches are really the easiest of all our trips. We always see whales...always! And the people are usually in a good mood. Cruise control here I come!

On both trips we had breaching whales and bubble net feeding whales and tons of sea lions and eagles! It was a great day on the water.

I finished up about 5 p.m. and headed for the house. Cindy was working late on a special project so she would not be home until about 6:30 p.m. or so.

I sat down in my chair with a cold beer and reached for the TV remote when my phone rang but it was not a regular call. It was a Facetime call...you know the kind where you actually get to see the person on the line...video phones like we had been promised so many years ago! I'm still waiting for the flying cars though!

It was my nieces Jamie and Sara! They often Facetime me together when they are going out on the town...it is always the highlight of my day! I love them so much and I am truly blessed to have such a great relationship with them!

In unison they said, "Hey Unkie!"

"What are you girls doing?" I asked.

"We are going out to see Dale Watson play tonight!" Sara answered.

"Very cool! That sounds fun!" I said

biting my tongue as I said it...you see Dale Watson is an old school country singer and I really loathe country music but hey if they dig it good for them!

Jamie then said, "Hey I've had a couple of weird things that happened...one just now that I wanted to tell you about."

"Okay...what's up?" I asked.

"Well a couple of days ago I spotted this creepy dude following me." She continued, "He looks like a guy from back east...definitely not from around here! He followed me for about two hours at a mall and just kept staring at me. It was creeping me out. So I walked right up to him and asked him what the hell he was doing and he just stared at me. He would not say a word! So I gave him a good cussin' and told him I was going to call the police and then he just smiled at me really creepy-like. So I kicked him in the nuts as hard as I could! And he doubled over and called me a bitch! I told him to leave me the fuck alone and walked away. When I turned around he was gone. I thought that was the last I would see of him but tonight we decided to stop on the way to see Dale and have a pre-show cocktail at a bar on the way. Right after we ordered our drinks I spotted him again. He was standing in the corner staring at us again! Creepy!"

Sara said, "I really wanted to get out of there but we had just paid $10 each for drinks and really wanted to drink them! So we tried to ignore him and keep an eye on him at the same time...you know what I mean! And then these two big cowboys started hitting on us and we got distracted...well I got distracted because they were kinda cute."

Jamie added, "The boys wandered off for a second and I told Sara let's go run this asshole off! So we walked up to the guy and I yelled at him again. I told him I was going to call the cops if he didn't leave me alone and he smiled again so I kicked him in the nuts again! I could not believe he didn't see it coming a second time. When he was doubled over Sara shoved him into the wall. Just then the two cowboys showed up and asked if we needed a hand with this piece of shit and Sara said that we had it handled! The boys then laughed, grabbed the guy and carried him out to the parking lot where they proceeded to send him to the hospital! Sara and I snuck off to our car and got the hell out of there and now we are calling you."

"Wow! Are you still gonna call the police tomorrow?" I asked.

"Yes, but I don't think it will do any good. No way to identify him," she said.

"That is crazy! Do call the police! Are you still going out to the show?" I asked.

"I will call the police and no we are too freaked out so we are going home," she answered.

"I think that is a good idea! Please let me know if he comes back...not that I can do anything but I do want to know," I said.

"We will! We are almost home so we will let you go for now Unkie. We love you!" they finished the last part in unison again and we hung up.

When Cindy got home I told her the story and she was very concerned about the girls but I told her they would be fine…they can handle this no problem! But I too was very concerned because I knew that this goon worked for JD and what he was capable of doing. I really hoped those cowboys beat the living shit out of him!

JD Calls Again

It was a few lovely quiet days before JD called again. When I say "Quiet" I don't mean that the fishing was quiet because it most definitely was not!

The Coho were in and they were coming in huge numbers! We were killing the salmon during those few days!

It was truly crazy fishing...limits almost every trip. Not only did this make our customers happy it kept us so busy we didn't have time to think about anything else! Win win!!!

But this great streak was broken when JD did find my number again.

"Hello there, Captain…how are you today?" he asked.

"What do you want?" I snapped back.

"You know what I want!" he laughed and continued, "But first things first…your girls really did a number on one of my best men! He's gonna be out for three or four weeks!"

"If your best man got spotted and rolled by a couple of little ladies from Texas, I would say you might need to find some better men!" I said laughing.

"You may have a point…he was being reckless but that is not the point! You tell those little bitches to back off! If they do that again they are dead! You got that?" he growled.

Since I knew that he meant business I agreed, "I'll try to keep the wolves at bay."

"You fucking better! This really pissed me off! Oh and don't think that they are not being watched while he is in the hospital…I flew another man down the next day and he is all over them! Like stink on shit!" he said.

"I kinda figured," I said and continued, "By the way that last dickhead you sent me pulled a gun on me! That was not part of the deal!"

"Yeah he's been really unstable for a long time. That doesn't surprise me at all. But now you know...anything could happen when you are dealing with my special people! Keeps you on your toes!" he finished.

"Well that was not cool! It...," I started.

He interrupted, "Oh shut the fuck up! I'm not going to listen to your whining all day! Your next trip is Thursday at 5pm and I don't care if they catch a fish at all. Just take them out and shoot them and come back in...don't even put a hook in the water if you don't want to! This guy is the scum of the fucking earth! He turned on us...wore a fucking bug for the feds...the lowest of the low! So just make it a quick trip! His name is Cecil Byers and he will have his wife with him.

You will love her…she's a real treasure! Have fun, Captain!" and he hung up the phone.

I thought, "If he turned on you I like him! What in the world did he mean she's a real treasure? This could be interesting."

O Captain, My Captain...

A few days passed and it was the day of our next one way trip. I have to admit I was more than a little curious what JD meant when he said that Mr. Byer's wife was a "real treasure."

We got the boat ready and I headed up the dock...imagination running wild...but still hoping that I did not like these folks...it was a lot easier when that was the case. Anyway as I got to the top of the dock their taxi pulled in and the mystery started to be revealed.

Cecil Byers got out first and he was a

70'ish year old guy, very bald, and looked grumpier than hell! Truth be told he looked a lot like the comedian Jeff Dunham's puppet Walter! He never smiled...not even when I shook his hand...he just grimaced at me and grunted a bit.

Then came his wife Ophelia...,"Hi, Captain Kevin...oh you are a handsome man!" she continued. "I'm Ophelia but everyone calls me Phil!" She pushed my extended hand aside and hugged me like she was trying to jump my bones!

How should I describe Phil...she was mid-60's, round with thinning hair piled as high as she could get it, bright red lips, and drawn on eyebrows that looked like two checkmarks over her eyes! Drawn in a way so she constantly looked surprised!

As we turned to make our way down to the boat she latched onto my right arm with her left hand and simply would not let go! "Oh boy...got me a cougar with checkmark eyebrows...lucky me!" I thought.

Phil pointed out everything she saw on the way to the boat, "Cecil look there's an eagle!" she squealed.

"Grrr...I hate eagles! All they do is shit on things!" he responded.

"Oh Cecil...isn't that boat cute?" she asked.

"Boats are just floating holes you throw money into!" he grumped.

"And look at this...big strong Capt. Kevin's boat sure looks fast!" she announced.

"Looks like a crappy boat to me! I hate metal boats...no soul!" he said.

With that she leaned in close and whispered into my ear, "Just like him!" She giggled like a little girl!

I finally got her to let go of my arm and we got into the boat. As we shoved off Merik asked, "Where to today?"

"Halibut Cove area...should be some good salmon there now!" I said.

"Sounds good!" he replied.

Once we got passed the "No Wake" zone I throttled her up and Phil chimed in, "O Captain…it's so powerful!" She reached over and put her hand on my knee and kept it there pretty much all the way to Halibut Cove.

When we got to the fishing grounds Merik went to work setting the gear and Cecil made his way onto the back deck…to complain and grumble.

Phil on the other hand would not leave my side!

I got up to go help Merik set the gear and she stood up in front of me and placed her hand on my chest and started to caress my chest and said, "O Captain, my Captain…I'm really enjoying this trip!"

"Uh…I kinda need to go help Merik," I said.

"But I kinda need you to help me," she said.

I thought, "It's hard to look seductive when your eyebrows just look surprised!"

"I promise…I'll come right back," I said.

"Well…I suppose…but I will miss you!" and with that she stepped aside. As I passed she grabbed a huge handful of my ass!

Merik was looking at me just as it happened and he smiled and shook his head!

Once the gear was down she summoned me again, "O Captain, my Captain… please come back!"

I looked at Merik with a look that said, "Please save me!" He returned my look with a slight shake of his head and the biggest shit eating grin I have ever seen!

I walked back into the cabin and sure enough she was back on me! I said, "Excuse me…I really need to drive the boat."

"Excuse me but I think you really need

to drive little ole me!" She made kissy faces at me.

Yep, JD was right a "real treasure"! What was killing me was the fact that her husband Cecil was completely unaffected by her behavior. I was beginning to think he was just glad it was someone else's turn!

Well the caresses and the ass grabs and the kissy faces continued for another couple of hours and the whole time poor Merik was stuck with Mr. Sourpuss Grumpypants who remained that way even when he was catching fish!

I was starting to worry a bit...if she never leaves the cabin there is no way for me to get the 9mm out to do the deed. And at some point I was going to have to get to business. That's when she asked, "O Captain, my Captain, I'm afraid I'm going to need the little girl's room...where is it?"

I quickly pointed to the head and said, "It's right there and the door is on the back deck."

She made another kissy face and said, "I'll miss you!" and made her way to the head.

This was my chance...I grabbed the gun and made my way to the back deck. There was another boat about a mile and a half up the channel from us but I had to take the chance.

I shot Cecil in the back of the head...he never knew what hit him and he slumped onto the deck.

She then came out of the head and I finally got to see what her surprised face really looked like. It looked exactly the same as her non-surprised face and I shot her right then and there.

We went right to work with our usual tasks and planted them off of Eagle Reef in about 450' of water.

For the first time we actually talked on the way back in...I guessed we were starting to accept the new normal.

"Boy he sure was a grumpy old bastard wasn't he?" I asked.

"No shit! And she was all over you!" he laughed.

"Ha...yeah Granny the Groper was indeed all over me! You were jealous! I could tell!" I said.

"No way! That shit was gross! I had to watch it happen and it disturbed me!" he said.

"It disturbed you? You should've been on the receiving end! But then again...you know what they say...any lovin' is good lovin'!" I said.

Merik just shook his head and laughed, "That is so wrong!"

"Let's go home." And we did just that.

Plans And Dreams

In between trips a few days later Merik and I started to discuss the possibility of what we would do if we actually did manage to find a way out of our current situation. Even though neither of us had been able to come up with even a plausible option at that point.

"So…when this is over do you have any ideas as to what you want to do?" I asked.

"I just want to disappear! Head down south and start over if I can," he said.

"Yeah, I've thought about that too. Have you spent any of the money yet?"

"No! Not even a penny! I've got it hidden

and no one knows where but me! It's gonna stay there until I leave," he said.

"Yeah...mine too. Gonna be fun to try to launder it though when the time comes! Not like we can just start spending money all willy-nilly...that would draw attention quick!" I said.

"Yeah...I've thought about that too. You know there is one thing I would really like to do...it's probably silly but I would really like to use some of the money for my buy in for the World Series of Poker in Vegas!" he said.

"That is not silly at all! I say do it! When will you have another chance! How much is the buy in?" I asked.

"It's only ten grand...I could easily say that I had saved that much up over the last couple of seasons!" he replied.

"Well then I say, Go Get 'Em!" with a laugh.

He laughed too and the phone rang and of course it was JD there to spoil our lovely day.

"You ready for another lovely trip there, Captain?" he asked.

"Not really!" I stated.

"Well tough shit there homeboy! I'm sending you a lovely couple from southern California...Danny Sullivan and Shayne McGuire. The trip will be Saturday at 5 p.m. and I want them to have a four hour whale trip. They are photographers and they want whales. I know whale trips can be tough but who am I kidding...I don't fucking care! Have fun with them! They own a limo service that we have used for years and they work really hard so I thought they needed a vacation!" he said laughing.

"What a guy!" I said.

"Why yes I am! Oh and when you are done save their cameras for me...I really love their photos! Very talented! Talk to you soon!" and he hung up.

"Joy oh joy!" I thought.

The Photographers

"What will we get today?" I thought.

Hardcore photographers tend to be very difficult to please because they want it all! They want bubble net feeding whales, jumping whales, whales showing good tail, whales that perform right on cue, whales that strike and hold that perfect pose, constant action and no other boats in their shots! Yeah, that is pretty much what they want so whale trips with hardcore photographers can be challenging to say the least.

"Well if they turn into dicks it will make the end of the trip a whole lot easier!" I quietly said under my breath as I made my way up the dock to get our guests.

They arrived right on time as usual and they started to unload the taxi. Wow! They had a lot of gear for just two people. Four camera bags and two gear bags and another bag with a laptop inside…oh well here we go.

Danny had a slender build with bright red hair and an inviting smile and laugh.

Shayne kinda surprised me…when she got out of the taxi…I had expected a dude. She struck me as slightly weary and cautious when it comes to strangers. Not a "Stranger Danger" type…just guarded. "She probably will warm up after she gets to know us," I thought.

Well we made it down to the boat and

started our trip. Since we had four hours I decided to run out to the Lizard Head area...it was a lot further than the other whale boats could go so it should be easier to do the deed out there and I had heard some good reports of a group of bubble net feeding whales in that area.

I was quite surprised to not encounter any animals to speak of as we rounded South Shelter and even more surprised when we did not see any all the way to Pt. Retreat. I was starting to get worried there would not be any out at Lizard Head either.

Just then Shayne started to grumble, "Hey why aren't we seeing any whales? Do you even know where they are? Danny, I told you to let me book the whale trip!"

"No worries...they are just up ahead. I have info on where they are and the good news is there should not be any other boats there to," I said.

"Well that would be good," She continued. "Danny where is my polarizer? Where is my damn polarizer? I told you to bring it! Where is it?"

"Shayne...it's in the blue bag. Let me get it for you," he answered giving me a smile and a wink.

We ran for about another twenty minutes and truth be told I was really starting to sweat...still no whales! When Merik announced, "Thar she blows!" as he pointed up ahead of us.

Sure enough there was a spout and another spout and another and three more! There those beautiful things were...all would be well!

About five minutes later I pulled back the throttle as the whales set a beautiful bubble net about a hundred and fifty yards off our port side.

Danny and Shayne made their way to the back deck with their cameras and I'm tellin' you the back of our boat looked like the sideline of the Superbowl! Biggest damn lenses I had ever seen.

A juvenile humpback breached and

Shayne said, "Damn it…I wasn't ready?"

It breached again and she started to fire then she yelled, "Danny! You are in my shot! Get out of my shot!"

This type of exchange went on periodically for the next couple of hours.

The whales took a long dive and everything got really quiet for about thirty minutes and I was hoping that they had not buggered off as they sometimes like to do when they are either full or are having a hard time finding another school of bait to eat!

Danny said, "I know what to do…time for a whale dance!" and with that he jumped up on the bow and started dancing and chanting to the whales!

"Whale…show us your tail! Give us some tail! We want some tail!" he continued, "Shake your money maker! Jump whales jump!"

We were all laughing so hard they both missed the shots when the whales surprisingly did come up!

The next time the whales went down Danny grabbed a handful of blue M&M's and started throwing them overboard.

"What the heck are you doing?" I asked.

"They are for the whales! Whales love blue M&M's!" he announced with a batshit crazy laugh that cracked us all up.

"Wow...this dude is nuts!" I thought.

But then the whales came back up and they were headed right for us! I left the boat in neutral and they swam all around us. It was amazing!

The shutters were flying at that point. This was going to be the highlight of the trip so I quietly pulled my trusty 9mm out of my red bag...a whale sprayed Danny in the face with its breath and he screamed, "That whale just blew me!" and I drew down on him in the bow of the boat and shot him in the back of the head. He almost fell overboard...I had to grab him to keep him in the boat.

I then turned and quickly made my way

to the back deck only to find that Shayne was still photographing the whales! She was completely oblivious to the fact that I had just shot her husband on the bow! I quickly dispatched her in the same way I had done Danny and we went to work.

On the way back I asked Merik to clean up the cameras as well as the boat. He did and he started messing with Shayne's camera and was able to pull up the pictures she had taken and they were amazing to say the least. He then took Danny's camera and found those equally amazing.

"I guess we now know why JD wanted those cameras," Merik said.

I looked at him and said, "Fuck JD!"

He just nodded.

The Exit Strategy

As we were pulling into the harbor late that evening I noticed two guys in suits standing on the dock in the vicinity of our slip...this seemed odd. You see the only people that wear suits in Juneau are legislators or people from out of town. We don't even wear suits to weddings or funerals...just jeans, Carhartts, and always XtraTufs. If you are in a suit you are obviously up to something!

So seeing these out of place dudes on our dock at 9 p.m. gave me pause so I reached into my red bag, pulled out the 9mm and put it on the dash behind my radar...just in case.

I swung the boat around the end of our dock and made my way to our slip. One of the out of place guys was standing at our slip and he slowly turned around. I'll be damned if it was not JD!

I instantly thought, "What the hell does he want? This can't be good!"

I slid the boat to a perfect stop in our slip, Merik jumped out and tied us up.

I opened the front door to access the bow of the boat and stepped halfway out as to have one foot on the bow and one inside the cabin…giving me full access to the 9mm if I needed it.

"Hello there, Captain!" JD said. "Do you have my cameras?"

"What the hell?" I asked, "Did you just come here for those stupid cameras? Yes, I have them you piece of shit!"

He started to laugh and I took a quick look around to assess the situation. Over JD's left shoulder about twenty feet away was the other stranger in the suit…he looked just like I had envisioned all of his goons to look. Slicked back black hair, pinstripe suit, dark sunglasses even though it was 9 p.m. and the sun was waning. Then I quickly glanced over at Merik...he was standing just to the right of me with one hand on the top rail of the boat and a cold look in his eye I had never seen before...there was a slight line of sweat appearing on his brow and I could sense his rage, fear, and pure unadulterated hatred for the piece shit that was standing in front of him. Just above his head I spotted something I really did not want to see...Capt. Ben was standing in the cabin of a boat about four slips over watching all of this play out.

"Damn it!" I thought and I turned back to look square at JD.

"You silly man...I'm not just here to pick up my cameras," he laughed. "I'm here to discuss your exit strategy. I'm beginning to think it might be time for you to retire."

My blood ran cold and my heart tried to leap out of my chest! I knew what that meant and I was not having any of it!

"Yeah, I know what you have in mind for our exit strategy. You want to send us on a vacation!" I shouted.

I glanced at Merik and he at me and the look said everything I needed to know! And we both looked back at JD.

JD laughed again, "Yeah, you're right! The two of you really look like you need a vacation. Where would you like to go? Bungee jumping in New Zealand, skydiving in Vegas, or scuba in Grand Cayman? You name it and I'll make it happen!"

"We pirates are always most dangerous when we are backed into a corner!" I thought. "The outcome is inevitable… just do it!"

"JD…I have my own exit strategy!" I calmly but forcefully stated doing my best Samuel L. Jackson imitation.

He chuckled, "And just what is that strategy?"

I quickly grabbed the 9mm and pointed it at him and shouted, "This Mother Fucker!" shooting him three times right in the chest!

He stumbled back a step or two and dropped to his knees with a look of total disbelief on his face as he tried to get his gun out of his jacket and he shouted, "Jackson! Kill him! Kill him now!"

And Jackson replied, "No JD...I don't think so!"

JD tried to turn to look at Jackson and as he did I shot him in the side of the head and he dropped to the dock with a twisting motion.

I trained the gun on Jackson, "Don't move or I will kill you too!" I shouted.

"Don't shoot!" he yelled. "Thank you for freeing us all!"

This statement really confused me and I thought, "He's trying to trick you!"

"I have to text the boys," he said.

"No fucking way! If you text them they

will kill our families!" I shouted

"If I don't text them they will kill them so I have to let them know that JD is dead!" he continued. "My cell is in the right front pocket on my jacket...my gun is under my left arm under the jacket...I have to reach into my pocket to get my phone...are you going to let me do that?"

"Go ahead but any other moves and I will kill you!" I said.

He nodded and slowly moved his right hand toward his pocket. As it disappeared into that pocket my anxiety doubled...no tripled! He slowly pulled out that hand along with his iPhone. He then began to type out a message and he spoke as he typed, "JD is dead! Leave them alone! We are free!"

"I'm going to hit send now." He said.

"No!" I shouted. "I don't believe you! I think you just told them to kill everyone!"

"Come here, Merik," he said. "I'll show you what I typed."

"No! Merik you stay right there!" I shouted again. "It's a trap! He's gonna try to grab you for a shield! You can toss the phone to Merik and he will look at it!"

With that he slowly and deliberately tossed the phone to Merik. He caught it and read out loud, "JD is dead! Leave them alone! We are free!"

Jackson then said, "Go ahead and hit send Merik."

"No! It could be a bomb! Toss it back to him and let him blow himself up!" I said.

"Wow! You really are paranoid! But I suppose it stands to reason! Toss me the phone," he said.

Merik did, Jackson hit send and nothing happened. Then his phone went crazy! Ding! Ding! Ding! And he read each text message out loud... "Really?" "Thank God!" "I'm out of here!"

He then said, "You have solved all of our problems! No one else was ever brave enough to actually do it! But you still have one problem left to deal with!"

"What is that?" I asked.

He calmly pointed down at JD's body and said, "That piece of shit!" and he turned and started to walk away.

"Hey! Aren't you gonna help us with this?" I asked.

"Nope! I'm done with this life! You know what to do!" as he quickly sprinted up the dock.

I looked over at Merik and nodded. I jumped out of the boat and we each grabbed an arm and started to drag JD to the back deck when all of a sudden he became a lot lighter! We turned and Ben had picked up his feet and was helping us.

"Ben...this is not your problem! Go away and forget everything you saw!" I said.

"Fuck that! It's my problem now! Let's do this!" he stated.

"Thank you!" I said and we loaded JD onto the back deck.

Ben told Merik to hose off the dock and while he did so Ben untied the boat. As soon as Merik was done they both jumped in and we shoved off.

As we made our way through the harbor I started fumbling for my phone... "Have to check on everyone!" I thought.

Ben said, "Hey Muchacho, why don't you let me drive so you can call your family?"

I looked at him and agreed that was a good idea!

He said, "You don't look like you should be driving a boat. Besides I know right where to go to get rid of a piece of shit!"

With that I got up and gave him the helm and called Cindy.

"Hey...are you okay?" I asked.

"Yeah just waiting for you to come home!" she said.

"Good! We are having a little issue with the boat....gotta fix it tonight so I will be home in a few hours...sorry!" I said.

"Is everything okay?" she asked.

"Oh it will be soon!" I said. "No worries! See you soon!"

I then sent text messages to Sara and Jamie and they both responded with "It's after midnight! This is just great my uncle is drunk texting me! Go to bed! Love you!"

And with that I decided I didn't need to text mom…I had a feeling she was alright. But I did text Dan that he could stand down. All was well! And he replied with a smiley face.

Merik checked with his family and they were all safe as well.

Then Ben asked, "So…what the fuck was that all about?"

So I proceeded to tell him the whole story and this was the second time since this whole mess had started that I got to feel a catharsis and it felt damn good!

When we got to the middle of Lynn Canal we tied all the extra downrigger balls we had to JD's legs and lowered him into the drink. When we let him go and he started to sink down to the bottom, the feeling of relief really started to sink in for both Merik and I.

Ben said, "We are really running out of daylight fast...can I open her up on the way back in and see what she will do? I've really wanted to do that since you repowered her with those twin 150's!"

"Ha! Go for it!" I laughed. "Blow the fucker up! I really don't care!"

He dropped the hammer and we were back in Auke Bay in about twenty minutes.

We tied up the boat and made our way up the dock. At the top I said, "Hey, thanks for the help! Not sure how I can repay you?"

He said, "Don't worry about it! I know the old three S rule...Shoot, Shovel and Shut up!"

We laughed and he got in his truck and drove off.

Merik asked, "Do you think we can trust him? I mean we have a lot hanging out there right now."

"Merik…he just helped us hide a body. He's now one of us…he is part of it! We can trust him!" I said.

He nodded in agreement.

I opened my truck door and there were our two envelopes for the photographers' trip but they seemed a bit larger than usual. There was also a note under them that said, "Thanks again for freeing us all! There is a little extra in the envelopes for each of you."

"See you tomorrow!" I said to Merik and I drove home as fast as I could. I walked in and hugged and kissed Cindy and relaxed just a bit more.

The next day I slipped an envelope with a hundred grand into Ben's truck with a note that said, "Thanks!"

The Next Chapter

About a week later…once I really started to believe that the nightmare was truly over. I arranged to get off early and went home and picked up Cindy for a picnic out the road to watch the sunset.

We stopped at the store and procured some nice olives, crackers, salumi, cheese, smoked salmon, grilled artichokes, and a nice bottle of red wine.

We drove out the road laughing and talking all the way out to Eagle Beach where we decided to have our picnic.

We rolled down the windows...it was a lovely evening...just warm enough to be comfortable but you could tell that summer would soon be over.

We nibbled and sipped wine and chatted and enjoyed the view of the Chilkat mountain range across the canal from us.

"Cindy...I think it may be time for us to make a big change. What do you think?" I asked.

"I don't know...I'm still enjoying living here," she said.

"Yeah me too but you know we are not getting any younger and I've been thinking a lot about Ireland," I said.

We had been toying with the idea of chucking it all...just like we did when we moved to Alaska all those years ago...and buying a pub in Ireland. It was definitely a recurring dream we both had pondered for many years.

She said, "Oh...I might be talked into that...are you really serious?"

"Yeah, I am this time. I have been rat holing some money for years"...she still did not know about the nightmare that we had just gone through and she never would if I could help it. Nor did she know about all the money that I had stashed. "We could sell the boat and that just might cover the cost of a small pub. What do you think?" I finished.

"This is so funny!" she said. "I've been surfing properties in Ireland for about a month for fun! So if you are serious I say yes!"

"Perfect! Let's do it! I'll put the boat on Craigslist at the end of the season," I said.

We told our family and friends about our big plan and they all thought we were crazy! Except of course Jamie and Sara and they said they would be there to visit as soon as we had a place.

Truth be told I really was not done with Alaska but I thought it best that we move on. Too much rough water this last summer for me. Besides I figured getting lost overseas might keep us a little safer.

So we got the ball rolling and the boat sold surprisingly fast. We then sold everything that we could except of course for the things that really meant a lot to us. Cindy found a great little pub in county Wicklow and we were off.

Merik too decided it was best to change his location and he moved down to the Seattle area. But he didn't keep quite as low a profile as we did…he did take some of his money and buy into the World Series of Poker in Vegas. The first year he made it to the second day and won back his entry fee before getting knocked out and the next year he won the whole damn thing!

I still do miss Alaska from time to time as does Cindy. We miss the beauty, the sea, the mountains, the people, the fishing, and the whales. Who knows maybe we will find ourselves there again. Maybe we could take a cruise! Wouldn't that be rich!

J. Kevin Burchfield

ABOUT THE AUTHOR

J. Kevin Burchfield loves living the Alaskan dream! As a fishing guide he enjoys sharing The Great Land's beauty and adventure with friends, family, and anyone else brave enough to share his passions.

He makes his home in beautiful Juneau, Alaska. There he loves to fish, hunt, fish, whale watch, brew beer, drink beer, fish, and dream with his wife Cindy and their dog Moose.

J. Kevin Burchfield

Other books by this author...

Jingle-Jingle
(J. Kevin Burchfield)

Full Moon Over Juneau
(J. Kevin Burchfield)

The Great Alaskan Adventure...
with Zombies!
(J. Kevin Burchfield)

Rip Some Lips
(J. Kevin Curry)

How to Piss Off and Alienate the World
(J. Kevin Curry)

Available at fine bookstores and at
www.jkevinburchfield.com

J. Kevin Burchfield

The book is over!

Put it down!

Now go outside and go fishing or brew some beer or drink some beer!

Are you still holding this book? Don't make me come over there! I will you know! You've just read this book so you know what I'm capable of...you have been warned!

J. Kevin Burchfield

Sleeps With The Fishes

Made in the USA
San Bernardino, CA
27 April 2016